The Butterfly Ride

By Amy Ackelsberg
Illustrated by Saxton Moore

Grosset & Dunlap
An Imprint of Penguin Group (USA) Inc.

GROSSET & DUNLAP
Published by the Penguin Group
Penguin Group (USA) Inc., 375 Hudson Street,
New York, New York 10014, USA
Penguin Group (Canada), 90 Eglinton Avenue East, Suite 700,
Toronto, Ontario M4P 2Y3, Canada
(a division of Pearson Penguin Canada Inc.)
Penguin Books Ltd., 80 Strand, London WC2R 0RL, England
Penguin Group Ireland, 25 St. Stephen's Green, Dublin 2, Ireland
(a division of Penguin Books Ltd.)
Penguin Group (Australia), 250 Camberwell Road, Camberwell, Victoria 3124, Australia
(a division of Pearson Australia Group Pty. Ltd.)
Penguin Books India Pvt. Ltd., 11 Community Centre,
Panchsheel Park, New Delhi—110 017, India
Penguin Group (NZ), 67 Apollo Drive, Rosedale, Auckland 0632, New Zealand
(a division of Pearson New Zealand Ltd.)
Penguin Books (South Africa) (Pty.) Ltd., 24 Sturdee Avenue,
Rosebank, Johannesburg 2196, South Africa

Penguin Books Ltd., Registered Offices:
80 Strand, London WC2R 0RL, England

ISBN 978-0-448-45732-1   10 9 8 7 6 5 4 3 2 1

On this day, just like any other day, Orange Blossom was working in her store. "I always do the same things," Orange said with a sigh. "I wish something exciting would happen. Sometimes Berry Bitty City is so boring!"

3

That afternoon, Orange met her friends at Strawberry Shortcake's café for a snack. "I think we should go on an adventure!" she told them.

"That's a great idea, Orange!" said Lemon Meringue.
"What do you have in mind?" asked Blueberry Muffin.
"I'm not sure . . . ," replied Orange.

"How about a ride on Lemon's boat?" Raspberry Torte suggested.
"Hmmm," said Orange, "we did that last week."

"Maybe we could go on a hike," said Plum Pudding.
"I don't think so," said Orange. "I want to do something new and berry special!"

"I know!" exclaimed Orange. "How about a butterfly ride?"
"Yes!" cried her friends.

"Now that sounds like a berry great adventure!" said Strawberry.
"I know just the butterflies who can take us!" said Lemon. "Come on!"

The girls found the butterflies and hopped on.

"Please take us somewhere berry exciting!" Orange told her butterfly. Then she held on tight as the butterfly fluttered its wings and took off, leading the way.

The butterflies soared high above Berry Bitty City.
"Oh, look!" cried Plum. "Everything seems so tiny from up here!"
"Blueberry, I can see your bookstore!" said Lemon. "It's berry bitty!"

"And there's the berry patch!" said Raspberry. "Look at how the berries sparkle in the sunlight!"

"It's beautiful!" exclaimed Strawberry.

Next, the girls flew through a field of puffy dandelions. As the butterflies zipped in and around the puffs, the seeds went everywhere.

"It's like we're flying through a snowstorm!" cried Orange.

The friends flew all afternoon. When they got tired, they stopped and shared a picnic with the butterflies. As they ate, the sun began to set over Berry Bitty City.

"What a fruitastic day!" exclaimed Raspberry.
"This was a perfect adventure!" agreed Orange.

"It's getting late," said Strawberry. "We should get home before it becomes dark."

As her friends got on their butterflies and took off, Orange stayed behind. She didn't want to leave.

Orange imagined what it would be like if she didn't have her
own shop and could fly on a butterfly every day.

Or better yet, what it would be like if she lived in the forest instead of in Berry Bitty City. She could swing in the trees and eat juicy fruit straight from the vines.

But then Orange realized that if she lived here, she would be all by herself. It wouldn't be any fun without her berry best friends!

Suddenly, Orange noticed that Strawberry, Blueberry, Plum, Raspberry, and Lemon were riding away.

"Wait for me!" cried Orange.

"Is everything okay?" Blueberry asked when Orange had caught up.

"I didn't want to come home yet," Orange explained. "But now I know that new adventures are only a butterfly ride away from home!"